DAVE KEANE

Joe Sherlock

KID DETECTIVE

Case #000003:

The Missing Monkey-Eye Diamond

HarperCollinsPublishers

J

Joe Sherlock, Kid Detective, Case #000003:
The Missing Monkey-Eye Diamond
Copyright © 2006 by David J. Keane
address HarperCollins Children's Books, a division of HarperCollins
Publishers, 1350 Avenue of the Americas, New York, NY 10019.
www.harpercollinschildrens.com

Library of Congress Cataloging-in-Publication Data
Keane, David, 1965–
    The missing monkey-eye diamond / Dave Keane.— 1st ed.
        p. cm.— (Joe Sherlock, kid detective ; case #000003)
    Summary: During a neighbor's chaotic wedding day, a super-sleuth
fourth grader solves the case when the wedding ring goes missing.
    ISBN-10: 0-06-076191-1 (trade bdg.)
    ISBN-13: 978-0-06-076191-2 (trade bdg.)
    ISBN-10: 0-06-076190-3 (pbk.)
    ISBN-13: 978-0-06-076190-5 (pbk.)
    [1. Rings—Fiction. 2. Weddings—Fiction. 3. Mystery and detective
stories.] I. Title. II. Series.
PZ7.K2172Van 2006   2006000556
[Fic]—dc22   CIP
                                                              AC

Typography by Christopher Stengel
1 2 3 4 5 6 7 8 9 10
❖
First Edition

For Karen Beaumont,
with gratitude

—D.K.

Contents

· Chapter One ·
Super Soaker

THE GREAT DETECTIVE

There's nothing better than a boiling hot bathtub to ease the boredom I feel between cases.

Although I'm just at the start of my career as a detective, I've been solving mysteries since I only had one tooth and drooled like a waterfall. Waiting for the next case has always been the toughest part of life behind the magnifying glass.

Waiting also drove Sherlock Holmes nuts.

Mr. Sherlock Holmes was the best dang detective to ever put his pants on one leg at a time. And like The Great Detective, I've dedicated my life to solving mysteries. So I spend lots of time waiting.

But boredom is just one of the reasons I'm boiling myself like a yam on a perfectly good Saturday afternoon.

The other reason is that my first violin recital begins in exactly three hours and fourteen minutes. Making matters worse is the fact that I've only had eight lessons—and I sound like it.

Sadly, just as I'm beginning to feel slightly relaxed, I burf.

"Burf" is a word invented by my best friend, Lance Peeker. As Lance will gladly explain to you, the word "burf" comes from combining the words "barf" and "burp."

Basically, a burf happens when you burp so big and throaty that some of the hot, sour stuff from your stomach comes flying up your windpipe and sprays into the back of your throat. Usually it's just about a teaspoon (according to Lance's estimates), but it can

ruin your whole day. Especially when it tastes exactly like something you ate the day before.

Unfortunately for me, my burf has the distinct odor and taste of an egg salad sandwich. This is surely the worst thing on the planet to burf.

Trust me.

Even worse, it's been over two days since I ate that hideous sandwich.

As I try to choke down the teaspoon of half-digested egg salad sandwich, I hear my little sister, Hailey, giving what sounds like a tour of our house.

"And this is our hallway," Hailey's muffled voice explains from behind the door. "And see this big pink stain here on the carpet? It's from the time Sherlock ate a family-size bag of cheese puffs and threw up like a volcano. You can still smell it on warm days."

"Interesting," a grown-up's deep voice responds.

I sit up in alarm, sloshing water all over the floor. What's going on out there? Who is my sister talking to? Why in the world is she talking about my throw-up stains?

"Of course, Sherlock *wanted* to throw up in the bathroom," my sister continues, "but my sister, Jessie, wouldn't let him in. She can't stand him."

I hear my sister start to jiggle a screwdriver around in the bathroom door's lock. My eyes search crazily for my towel, but it's on the other side of the bathroom. I start to sweat—even though I'm still in the bath! *How is that even possible?*

Hailey's voice cackles on the other side of the door. "My dad says the only way to get a stain like that out is with a pair of scissors."

To my absolute horror, the lock suddenly releases with a click and the door swings wide open.

Hailey bursts into the bathroom, followed by an enormous man wearing a tight-fitting tuxedo.

I am quite certain that this will go down in history as one of the weirdest moments of my life.

"Sherlock, sorry to interrupt your scuba-diving expedition, but Mr. Castro here needs a detective fast," Hailey says with a sweeping, dramatic hand gesture. "So make like a knuckle and get crackin'!"

I cover myself with my big sister's Girl Chat Sleepover sponge. I am breaking new ground in the embarrassment department.

Sure, I'm furious at my little sister. In

fact, I'm ready to strangle her. But I can't help but feel a great sense of relief, too. Finally, my third case as a private detective has arrived.

"Sherlock, you must help my son! Something terrible has happened," Mr. Castro booms from the end of the bathtub.

"I see," I say, as if considering the terribleness of the thing that has happened, but I'm really thinking that I should have taken a bubble bath.

"Gross! It smells like a rotten egg salad sandwich in here," my sister says in a goofy, high-pitched voice. She's gotten a whiff of my burf. She holds her nose and stumbles around like she's been hit with a poison dart.

"Somebody please tell me that's not my bath sponge!" warbles a shrill voice from somewhere behind Mr. Castro. It's the voice of my always-angry big sister, Jessie. "I'm telling Mom you're using my stuff, and she'll make you buy me a whole basket of new bath sponges, you little freak!" Jessie pushes her way into the bathroom and stands like a bull snorting at one of those guys who twirls around a red blanket.

She doesn't even say hello to Mr. Castro.

"Who's having a party in the bathroom?" It's my dad. He, too, has somehow worked his way through the doorway. "And look, Mr. Castro is here! Hey, are those eggs I smell?"

"Did Sherlock throw up again?" my mom calls out from somewhere in the hallway.

I'm practically expecting my grandparents to come crawling through the window.

Sensing the need for crowd control, my mom starts clapping her hands together. "Okay, everyone out of the bathroom! Let Sherlock get his robe on and talk to Mr. Castro in the living room."

Thank goodness for my mom. And thank goodness the long wait for my next case is over.

• Chapter Three •
Making a Molehill
into a Mountain

MR. CASTRO'S HAND **=** Joe Sherlock's HEAD

Mr. Castro is not just a large man; he's like five men for the price of one. With a head as big as a prize-winning pumpkin and a body like a three-story building, he looks like he's about to explode through the seams of his tuxedo.

As I stand dripping in front of him, I can't help but stare at his enormous hands. Each finger is like its very own breakfast burrito.

"Sherlock, I am in the most dire situation you can imagine," Mr. Castro begins in his foghorn voice.

"Please, go on, Mr. Castro," I say, although I'm really thinking I have no idea what a "dire" situation is.

Mr. Castro's voice fills the room like rolling thunder. "My son is to be married at our house this evening. It's a madhouse down there. A last-minute scramble. It's buzzing like a beehive, with everyone rushing around doing final preparations. Sherlock, at six o'clock, over one hundred guests will arrive to watch my son get married in our backyard." He stops suddenly and stares at the palms of his mammoth hands, as if he can't believe how big his mitts have grown, either.

"That sounds just lovely," says Hailey. She must have snuck up behind me while Mr. Castro was speaking. Hailey sometimes helps me out on my cases, like an assistant. But actually, she's more like a stick in my mental mud.

"The reason I am here," Mr. Castro rumbles on, as if he hasn't even noticed Hailey's entrance, "is not so much my problem as it is the groom's problem."

"I see," I say, although I'm secretly kicking myself for not knowing what the heck a groom is.

"The groom is the guy who's getting married," Hailey whispers loudly in my ear, loud enough so that Mr. Castro knows that I have no clue what a groom is.

I give her some stink-eye and draw two fingers across my lips in a clear "keep that loud mouth of yours zipped shut" gesture.

"My son," Mr. Castro continues, looking up from his hands, "has misplaced the wedding ring and the very large and expensive diamond

Fumble!

that was attached to it."

"Fumble late in the fourth quarter!" exclaims Hailey so loud that my right eye twitches.

Suddenly the words come tumbling out of Mr. Castro like an avalanche of very large stones. "We've looked everywhere. The guests will be arriving soon. My son is in a panic. We're growing more desperate by the minute. Will you help us find the diamond ring, Sherlock?"

"You bet he will," Hailey announces, slapping me hard on the back.

I clear my throat, giving Hailey a glare that would surely melt cheese. "Um, I have my first violin recital tonight, Mr. Castro, but I think I can crack this case before I have to leave. This kind of thing is right up my alley."

Mr. Castro jumps to his feet very quickly for a man the size of a two-car garage. "Excellent! Please, there is no time to waste. I will pay any price you ask. Just come soon." He rolls past us and out the front door before I can even respond.

"Don't blow this one, Sherlock," Hailey says, slapping me hard on the back again. "It may be up your alley, but it looks like this one is way out of your league, big brother."

The three-headed jackrabbit bouncing around in my stomach tells me she might be right. Out of my league and out of my mind.

• Chapter Four •
Monkey See, Monkey Do

"I just don't think anyone will notice."

My mom is trying to convince me that I don't look like a complete doofus in the suit I wore last year at my aunt Peachy's fourth wedding. She wants me to wear it to the Castros' house in case I don't have time to get back here and change before we leave for my recital.

Sadly, I'm much taller than my pants seem to remember.

"I think you look like a spiffy little detective," she says, admiring me in a shaky voice that sounds like she's about to burst out laughing.

"Spiffy?" I groan. "I think you mean dopey."

"Maybe I can let the hem of those pants down a bit," she chuckles. "Let me get my sewing kit."

I grunt in exasperation. "Mom, I don't have time. The clock is ticking."

"Okay! Okay!" she says. Then she walks quickly away down the hall while covering her mouth with her hand. I think she's rushing off to find a nice quiet spot to have a good laugh at my expense.

"Holy shin extenders!" Hailey cries from behind me. "Did you take those pants off your Inspector Wink-Wink doll?"

"It's an action figure, not a doll," I mumble, staring up at the ceiling.

"Did Mom wash that suit in the microwave oven or what?" she giggles.

I sigh. "The pants are a little short."

"A little short? I can almost see your kneecaps." She has a good laugh, too. I'm so glad everybody is having the time of their lives.

I spin around to give her my two cents. "I don't need you to—" Suddenly I am frozen like a moose in the headlights. Hailey is wearing a fancy dress and swinging a little purse around in circles like some kind of deadly weapon.

"You can't come, Hailey!" I explode. "I don't have time to keep an eye on—"

"Oh, get off your high horse, Mr. Short Pants," she

interrupts. "Dad says I can go. And besides, you don't know the first thing about weddings. You didn't even know what a groom is. Boys are clueless when it comes to things like love and diamonds and manners and how to pour a cup of punch. So I'll just help out if you need me." « »

Before I can answer, Jessie snickers from the other end of the hall.

"Nice monkey suit, Detective Clam Digger," she snarls.

Hailey is at my ear in a flash. "Clam diggers are a kind of pants that women wear. They only cover three-quarters of the leg, just like your pants. . . . See, I'm already helping."

"I know that already," I whisper back, even

though I really don't. My head is starting to ache, and I haven't even left the house yet.

"I'm too busy for you right now, Jessie," I grumble.

"Aaaghgh," she grunts, which is how she responds to just about anything I say. It's the kind of sound typically made by someone who has a plastic fork stuck in their throat. Jessie is thirteen years old and has been in a bad

mood since she turned eleven. My dad says it's just a stage she's going through and that she'll grow out of it by the time she's thirty.

"I'm on a case right now and I don't have time to share a few laughs with you," I peep, although I wanted it to sound more like a snarl.

"Don't worry," she snaps, "your pants will provide all the laughs you need." She stops and considers me for a moment. "So what's the big mystery? Did someone steal your organ grinder?"

"Organ grinder?" I croak.

Hailey is at my ear in a flash. "An organ grinder is an old-fashioned street performer who turns a handle on a music box while a costumed monkey on a leash collects coins from people on the street. Jessie thinks you look like the monkey. That's already the second time I've—"

"We've gotta go!" I blurt out in exasperation. I pull Hailey down the hall and past Jessie. I give my sneering big sister the nastiest eye squint a kid wearing knickers can muster.

"Good luck on the case of the incredibly shrinking pants!" she calls after us.

Hailey starts in again. "She's saying that you're actually trying to solve the mystery of how your pants—"

"Just stop talking," I manage to hiss before another burf escapes.

"Yikes! You stink like dead lizards!" Hailey screeches.

"It's egg salad sandwich," I say.

"That is just so gross," she gasps, grabbing her nose.

"Hailey, please stop talking!" I feel like pulling out my hair, but I don't have time. "I can't think with you blabbing away all the time. And there's something I need to do before we leave."

"I hope it involves taking a shower!" she exclaims in a plugged-up voice. She proceeds to stagger around, bump into walls, and shout, "Stink bomb! Stink bomb!"

With all these annoying distractions, I'm not sure I could think my way out of a wet paper bag. How am I supposed to solve a high-pressure mystery?

I need to do something I should have done as soon as Mr. Castro left our house. Maybe it's not too late.

• Chapter Five •
No Guts, No Glory

My best friend, Lance, never answers the phone. Ever.

Instead, Lance's grandma always picks up the phone, says something I can't understand, slams down the phone, and shuffles off to get Lance. It usually takes Lance about a week and a half to get to the phone.

While I wait for Lance, my mind wanders off in the direction of Mrs. Hudson.

Mrs. Hudson is my violin teacher. She is very strict. And very easy to disappoint. She's always yelling at me that the three most important factors in mastering the violin are repetition, repetition, and repetition. I know she thinks this is clever because every time she says it, she leans to one side and makes a creepy murmuring noise. In fact, she does this after she says just about anything. Now that I think about it, my violin teacher is completely nuts.

"Sherlock, you're green," Hailey says from across the room. "You're going to throw up, aren't you? It must have been that egg salad sandwich! I think it was toxic!"

"I'm on the phone," I grumble at her.

"I'll get a pot from the kitchen so you don't ruin another rug," she hollers. She runs off before I can stop her.

I signed up for violin lessons mostly because Sherlock Holmes is always playing the violin in his movies. It just happens to be my sort of luck that I get a wacko instructor who seems like she'd be better at running a maximum-security prison than teaching lazy kids to play the violin.

"Don't move," Hailey grunts from behind me. She's spreading newspaper out on the floor all around me. "Here's your target," she says, slamming down the enormous pot my mom uses to cook pasta. "I'll see if I can get some plastic sheets to cover the furniture!" she screams.

As I watch my panic-stricken sister scramble out of the room, it occurs to my stomach that I really should be practicing for tonight's recital. I need the work. I'm playing only two short songs at the recital, but when I play "Mary Had a Little Lamb" and "Farmer in the Dell," it sounds like three angry cats trapped in a dryer on fluff cycle.

Mrs. Hudson likes to say that I'm her most "challenging" student, which is just a nice way of saying she's met shellfish with more talent.

Just as Hailey rolls in my dad's industrial-strength shop vacuum from the garage, Lance finally picks up the phone.

"What took you so long?" I blurt into the phone.

"Sherlock? Hey, how'd your violin recital go?" he asks.

"It hasn't happened yet," I say. "It's tonight." I shift my feet around, and newspaper crinkles under my feet. "You're not coming, are you?"

"Sorry, pal, I'm as busy as a one-legged man in a tap-dancing contest."

I'm quiet for a few seconds. "Are you too busy to join me on my newest case? It involves a big diamond and a big payday. C'mon, Lance, I'll split the money with you if—"

"Uh, that sounds thrilling, but I entered this online *Vengeance in Venice!* tournament. I'm competing with thousands of players from around the world. Right now I'm playing some guy in India named Parth83."

I blow out some air. I look up at the ceiling and clench my teeth. I'm not surprised by his answer. Just surprised that I took the time to call him when I knew he wouldn't come. I need to accept the fact that Lance would rather play a video game with some strange kid in India than share an adventure with his best friend. "There's going to be lots of food," I say, and immediately wish I hadn't.

"Uh, that's great, but my grandma just made me some tuna nachos."

Tuna nachos? My stomach quivers at the thought. Those are two words that were never meant to be put next to each other! I turn around and lean over the pasta pot.

"He's gonna blow!" Hailey screams, and runs out of the room.

I hang up on Lance. I wait for the rolling sensation

in my stomach to pass. The phone rings in my hand. Without answering it, I know it's Mr. Castro, wondering what happened to me. I drop the phone into the pasta pot and stumble out our front door.

Sadly, I have no idea that the case waiting for me at the Castros' house will put my sleuthing skills and my sensitive stomach to the ultimate test.

• Chapter Six •
Living Room Weasel

Mr. Castro was right: His house looks like a swirling, whirling vortex of confusion and panic—a lot like our kitchen when my dad makes dinner.

The Castros live just six houses down from my house. It's usually the neatest house on Baker Street, with the most raked and clipped yard. But today it's taking a beating.

Mr. Castro is waiting for me at the open

front door. Without a word, he waves at me to follow him. I do.

The inside of Mr. Castro's home is a thunderous tornado of noise and confusion and fear that reminds me of lunch recess. It's hard to believe there will be a wedding here in ninety minutes.

"That's a terrific ice sculpture of a weasel," I shout over the noise, mostly to slow Mr. Castro down, since I'm practically running behind him now.

He stops and stares for a long time at the

MYSTERY ON ICE!

massive frozen sculpture that's being lowered by six men onto a long table.

"That's supposed to be a swan," Mr. Castro says with a weird look on his face.

"Oh . . . sometimes I get weasels and swans confused," I say awkwardly, cursing my brain for always being lost at sea when I need rescuing. But my explanation must satisfy Mr. Castro, because we're suddenly on the move again.

I quickly reach into my coat and feel my pad of paper and pencil. It's what I'll need to create one of the most important and useful tools of the successful detective: the time line.

You often see the main guy in detective movies use a time line to solve missing persons cases. I expect it works just as well for missing wedding ring cases.

As I jog in Mr. Castro's wake, my active

imagination can't help but cook up a few new nicknames for my large neighbor: The Walking Earthquake. The Human Skyscraper. Mr. Sun Block. The Man Who Ate Chicago. The Whole Enchilada. King Kong's Big Brother. The Shadow Maker. The Bouncer of Baker Street. All You Can Eat Man. Bigger Than—

Without warning, my nickname game is interrupted as a fear tucked in the back of my mind roars to life. It explodes so violently and unexpectedly that I think my bladder might pop. "Is Ranger here?" I ask, fearing a sneak attack by Mr. Castro's freakishly big and nasty dog, who has always wanted to snarf me down like a strip of crispy bacon.

"Ranger is staying at a relative's house for the day," he says as we make our way down a hallway. We stop before a closed door.

"Perfect," I say, but still check behind me just in case.

The Man Who Ate Chicago!

"Brace yourself," Mr. Castro warns. "Everybody is under a lot of stress."

"Of course," I say, trying my best to sound as confident as The Great Detective, but instead it comes out as a stuttering hiccup and gasp followed immediately by an explosive burf that almost blows me back through the door.

I secretly swear to never eat another egg salad sandwich for the rest of my life.

"Is somebody burning scrambled eggs?" cries a man who looks like a younger, equally gigantic version of Mr. Castro. "My eyes are watering!"

This, of course, is the groom. I study him as he checks the bottoms of his shoes for the source of the mysterious odor. Although he's dressed in a shiny tuxedo, he looks like a wreck.

Several strange men in tuxedos curse loudly and hurry to throw open the room's windows, as if they're desperate for any way to be useful.

The groom's eyes jump around the room wildly, like a guy trying to watch three tennis matches at the same time. I don't remember seeing him before, although he could almost pass for Mr. Castro's younger twin brother. He probably moved out of this house when I was no bigger than a loaf of bread.

"Son, this is the boy I mentioned," Mr. Castro says with a nod. "Sherlock, this is my son, Herbert Junior."

The men in the room look up briefly. My guess is they've never heard Mr. Castro's son referred to as Herbert Junior before. It's not the kind of name you want to get around.

Herbert Junior looks at me for the first time. He blinks. "What on earth happened to your pants?" he asks, as if he's momentarily forgotten his current difficulties and would rather focus on mine.

"Uh, it's a long story," I say with a fake laugh.

"Apparently not long enough," he huffs, and begins to pace back and forth and nervously run his fingers through his hair. "Kid, if you can get me out of this jam, you're a miracle worker."

"When was the last time anyone saw the ring?" I begin, pulling out the pad and pencil. I draw a simple line across my pad from left to right. This will be my time line.

"That diamond was huge!" the groom bellows just inches from my nose. I take half a step back. "How could I lose it on my wedding day?" he continues. "It was as big as a monkey's eye! How could this happen to me?"

Mr. Castro was certainly right about the stress taking its toll.

A tiny speck of the groom's spit has landed on my right eyelid. I'd love to wipe the thing off, but I'm afraid to make the slightest move. Instead, I try to imagine how big a monkey's eye might be.

GROOM'S SPECK O' SPIT!

Finally, the groom relaxes and sags a bit. He glances at his watch and returns to his pacing.

"So when was the last time you saw the ring?" I squeak, and clear my throat as if I can't figure out how my voice could squeak at a time like this.

In a sudden rush of words, the groom tells me that the last time he saw the ring was at the tuxedo shop this morning. He and his dad had gone in for some last-minute adjustments. "I showed my dad and the lady helping us the ring. The diamond was in a new setting, with a parade of little diamonds around it. That ring was worth more money than you and I will make in a lifetime, I guarantee you that much, Buster Brown."

"Interesting," I say after a pause, mostly because I can't think of why he thinks my name is Buster.

I carefully search all the pockets of the groom's jacket and pants. I even pull out my magnifying glass and inspect the cuffs at the end of his tuxedo pants, because I once found the missing key to my dad's briefcase in the cuff of his pants. It's a long shot, but you never know when you might strike gold—or diamond! The cuffs are empty.

I crawl around and give the room's carpet a close inspection as well. Nothing.

"Herbert Junior, I need a ride to the tuxedo shop as soon as possible," I announce, rising to my full height in this room full of giants. I now have their full attention. I am clearly their last hope—which sounds pretty desperate even to me. "It's best to begin at the start of the beginning."

The room goes silent.

"There isn't a moment to lose," I add, simply because it's something Sherlock Holmes always says in a pinch, and I need something to break the spell I've cast over them.

Then Mr. Castro clears his throat, spins around, and opens the door. "I will arrange your transportation with the limousine driver," he says, glancing down at his watch. "You are correct—we don't have a moment to lose."

Sherlock Holmes wasn't the kind of guy who needed Barf Blockers.

But I am.

The sad truth is that if I don't have a Barf Blocker pill before I get into a car, someone better have an empty shopping bag handy.

I suffer from extreme carsickness. Always have. I used to get carsick getting pushed around in a stroller. I get carsick just flipping through racing magazines at the dentist's office. In fact, if my dad backs the car down the driveway too fast, I'm usually blowing marshmallows by the time we clear the sidewalk.

Of course, there were no cars when Sherlock Holmes was a detective. He was always hopping into the back of these tiny black stagecoaches that would go clip-clopping down bumpy streets made of millions of rocks glued together. The bumping alone would have had me spewing in no time, but considering the horse poop plopping down all over the place, I don't know how the guy did it.

My stomach is already registering a 5.8 on the Sherlock Queasiness Scale, and I'm only walking down the hall behind Mr. Castro just thinking about getting my first ride in a limousine.

Hailey interrupts my thoughts by sticking a piece of cake in my face. Well, not actually in my face, but pretty darn close.

"The wedding cake is carrot cake!" she hisses. "Can you believe it? Nobody has carrot cake for a wedding reception. I hate carrot—"

"Are you nuts?" I snarl between clenched teeth. "Why on earth are you eating the wedding cake? The wedding hasn't even started! You're going to get me in big trouble!"

"Oh, take it easy, Mr. Daddy Longlegs,"

Hailey replies, as if taking a slice of a wedding cake before the wedding starts is no big deal. "It's just a smidge. And besides, I took it from way in the back, so nobody would notice. Can you believe it's carrot cake?"

"Give me that," I snap. I grab the fork from her. "Hide that plate and stay out of trouble. I'm

KRYPTONITE: NOT GOOD FOR SUPER POWERS

K

getting
a limo ride
over to the
tuxedo shop
where the groom
last saw the ring."

"A limo ride?" she says, and whistles. "Can I come?"

"No," I sigh. "You're like a poisonous hunk of kryptonite that weakens my supersensitive brain powers."

"Well, you better bring your cape so you can puke into it, Mr. Super Spew," she says. "You in the back of a limousine is something I'd love to see. Hey, don't forget your shopping bag."

"Just stay out of trouble," I grumble.

"Yes, sir, General Tiny Pants!" Hailey shouts, and salutes like an army guy.

As I growl and rush off to find Mr. Castro, I realize my little sister is less like an assistant and more like a speed bump for my brain.

Chapter Nine

A Stick in the Eye of the Storm

"**W**hat happened to your pants?"

The skinny girl standing in front of me in the Castros' living room is someone I think I know, but she's so covered in curls, ribbons, sparkles, and lip gloss that I can't quite place her.

"Do I know you?" I ask, squinting like some guy who's been whacked between the eyes with a wooden spoon.

"Silly Sherlock, it's me! Irene Adler!" she laughs.

"Oh," I mumble. "I didn't recognize you."

Irene Adler has given me the heebie-jeebies for as long as I can remember. Her most favorite hobby since preschool has been staring at me with her big, googly eyes. And she always stands next to me. Worst of all, she laughs at anything I say.

"What are you doing here?" I ask, trying to look past Irene at the swarm of activity going on in the Castros' home.

This question brings on a blast of laughter so loud that I duck like a guy who just heard a bullet whiz over his head. Her unexpected laughing always catches me by surprise. I am more certain than ever that there is something wrong with the wiring inside Irene Adler's head.

"I'm the flower girl, of course," Irene says,

and spins around, showing me her dress. "You must be the ring bearer." She giggles and punches me too hard on my arm. "It's almost like we're getting married, isn't it?"

I feel like someone just dropped a scorpion down the back of my pants.

"Ring bearer?" I gasp. "I don't even—"

Before I can finish, Hailey is at my ear again. My assistant can sneak up on me better than a ninja assassin with thick socks on.

"A ring bearer is sometimes part of a wedding ceremony," Hailey whispers in my ear. "He's usually this embarrassed, dressed-up kid who walks down the center aisle carrying a little pillow with the bride's ring tied to it. He follows the flower girl, who chucks rose petals all over the place.

Honestly, what would you do without me, Mister Peewee Pants?"

I start getting a sharp pain right behind my eyes.

The main guys in detective movies never seem to run into the kind of obstacles that I run into. And let's face it, Irene Adler is about as useful to me right now as a box of rocks. I need an escape plan and I need it fast.

"I've gotta go now, Irene . . . I've . . . I lost my monkey," I say, without thinking about what I'm saying while I say it.

"You have a monkey?" Irene howls with laughter and slugs me on the arm again. I can actually hear her lips crackling and smacking, like someone mixing a giant bowl of macaroni and cheese.

The needle on my internal creepometer is hitting the red zone. I officially have the willies.

"Well . . ." I say stupidly, momentarily wishing I had a brain that could think on its feet.

"You mean he *had* a monkey, until he lost it!" Hailey squeals with delight.

This only makes Irene laugh harder. She's in serious danger of sucking the ribbons right out of her hairdo.

Hailey puts her arm around Irene and steers her toward the house. "Let's see . . . where could Jimmy be?" Hailey says, pretending to look around while also naming my imaginary pet at the same time. She glances back at me and winks.

She's good. Maybe she's not such a bad—

"What happened to you?" a voice booms from behind me.

I flinch, spin around, and peep like a

recently hatched chick. It's Mr. Castro.

He looks down at my hand and slowly pulls Hailey's carrot-cake-encrusted fork from my clenched fist. *I should have gotten rid of that thing!*

"What's this?" he asks quietly.

"Uh . . . that? Oh, I found that in the bathroom just off the kitchen," I say with a shrug.

"We don't have a bathroom near the kitchen," Mr. Castro says, narrowing his eyes.

Dang it! Why am I the world's worst liar? I am caught like a hairy, fat fly in every single tangled web I weave. My stomach starts to do backflips.

He suddenly sighs, looking at the chaos going on all around us. "I've arranged everything with the limo driver," he says without looking at me. "Follow me. There's something I need to tell you."

Oh, great.

• Chapter Ten •
Limo Launch

"Sherlock!" Mr. Castro is staring at me like he can't believe his enormous eyes.

I realize he's been talking about something, but I haven't been listening. I'm distracted by the shiny limousine in front of me. I shake my head and downshift my brain into the here and now. My dang mind needs to be on a leash.

"Did you get that? Nobody can know what you're doing," Mr. Castro says, looking back over his boulder-size shoulders. "My wife can't know. The bride can't know. And my son's new in-laws certainly can't find out. It will start a panic that will spread like wildfire."

"Of course," I sputter, although I'm really thinking that I really don't know what an in-law is. Are the cops involved now?

"This is Earl," he says, motioning to the limo driver. Earl smiles and nods in my direction. "He was driving us earlier," Mr. Castro continues. "I've explained the urgency of the situation to him. He will retrace our steps for you until you locate the diamond."

Without a word, Earl pulls the back door open for me like I'm some big shot. I climb into the back of the vehicle with my stomach kicking and screaming the whole way.

Earl hops into the driver's seat and starts the engine. He seems like a pleasant enough man, but he wears large mirrored sunglasses, which I find irritating for some reason. I can see myself in his reflective lenses, sitting like a rich guy in the buttery-soft black leather. I wave at myself.

Earl waves back.

"Uh, hold on a moment," I say. I shift uncomfortably in my seat, and the leather makes an embarrassing noise. I shift a few more times so Earl knows that it was the leather seat and not me who made the noise. But, of course, no matter how much I squirm, the seat doesn't make another peep. Finally, I give up. "Um . . . I'd like to warn you that I have experienced some carsickness in the past."

"Yes, sir," he answers, and leans over in the seat. He fumbles around in the glove compartment and tosses back a box of Barf Blocker pills.

"Perfect," I exclaim, my eyes growing wide in amazement.

"Those also might help with your gas problem," he says as a wall slowly rises up between us. Before I can explain about the seat, the wall clicks into place, leaving me in silence.

I quickly pop in a pill and look around for something to drink. Of course, as my luck would have it, there's nothing to drink. In growing desperation, I spot a fancy bucket full of melting ice sitting on the seat across from me. But before I can snatch up the shimmering bucket, I experience what can only be described as liftoff.

I am thrown backward like I've been kicked by a school of mules.

I land upside down in the rear seat. On my head. I think. I can't be sure because I am almost instantly knocked out by the ice bucket, which has been launched from its resting place. It bounces squarely off my forehead. Then everything goes black. One half second later, I am shocked awake as the entire melted contents of the bucket explode all over me. I gasp in confused astonishment and clutch my throbbing forehead.

The lump above my eye is not the worst of my problems: The Barf Blocker pill has become wedged in my throat. And although it's a tiny pill, no bigger than a pencil eraser, I could swear that a speedboat has become stuck in my throat.

Gagging like a tortoise with a fur ball, I hold on for dear life. My stomach has forgotten everything it ever knew about car-sickness.

Just as my eyes notice the unused seatbelts, we stop. Suddenly. Very suddenly. I am once again sent rocketing through space and time. I hit Earl's wall of silence like a w e t bag of

walnuts.
   In the
sudden
silence, I hear
the whir of a small engine inside the seat.
The wall that separates us drops.
   "Here's our first stop," Earl announces.

• Chapter Eleven •
Calling on Mr. Spiffy

"I'd like to speak to Mr. Spiffy," I say with an amazing amount of authority considering my head has been dented by an ice bucket.

Mr. Spiffy's Tuxedo Emporium seems like a normal enough tuxedo rental store. As far as I can see, there is just one woman working at the moment, and there are no other customers in the store. Earl has chosen to stand out by the limo, perhaps in fear of my mysterious seat noises.

"There is no Mr. Spiffy here," says the woman. She is almost as short as she is wide, like a perfect square. She wears a measuring tape flung around her neck like a scarf. She also wears a pair of those half-glasses on the tip of her nose. As she looks me over, she can't seem to figure out if she should look at me through the half lenses or just over them. She tilts her head back and forth continuously as she tries to bring me into focus.

"When do you expect him back?" I ask.

Mr. Spiffy's TUXEDO EMPORIUM

NO CHECKS

"Never," she says with a puzzled look.

I rub the egg growing out of my forehead. "Is he sick?" I ask stupidly, mostly because I am completely distracted by her annoying head tilting.

"It's just a name, not a person," she says loudly and slowly, as if she's convinced I've had most of my brain removed for medical reasons. "There are twenty-two Mr. Spiffy formal wear stores. And there is no Mr. Spiffy at any of our stores. It's just a name someone thought up." She looks at me with pity.

"Mr. Castro sent me here," I say, deciding I'd better cut to the chase. "His son is getting married today. They were here earlier. He thinks he may have left something here, and he sent me to recover the item." It takes every ounce of concentration that my bruised and battered head can muster not to mention the missing diamond ring.

Her eyes grow wide. "It was like finding tuxedos to fit two redwood trees," she whispers, peering at me over her lenses. "Like Sasquatch, those men!"

Surprisingly, I know what she means. Lance is a Sasquatch expert.

In case you don't already know, Sasquatch is just a fancy name for Bigfoot, a shy and

hairy monster that roams around the forest leaving gigantic footprints everywhere. Lance has several books filled with very blurry photographs of him. There are also lots of pictures of scientists picking gross hair off tree trunks with tweezers. And a half dozen shots of hunters pointing at giant mounds of mysterious poop. Personally, I think it's just a guy in an ape costume with too much time on his hands.

Now that we've found some common ground, Mrs. Perfect Square is as helpful as a stepladder. She shows me the dressing rooms Mr. Castro and his son used. As I inspect the carpet, seats, and surrounding area with my magnifying glass, she tells me that she had to make several last-minute adjustments because their special-order XXXL tuxedos didn't fit quite right.

"They showed me the ring," she says,

tilting her head back so far I think she might fall over backward. "That diamond was bigger than a grape."

"Where did they put the ring?" I ask, trying not to sound too interested.

"Oh, I don't know," she says with a wave. "The younger one had it, I guess."

Mr. Spiffy's Tuxedo Emporium is a dead end. I hang my head in defeat. My gut tells me the ring is not here. It tells me I am running out of time. It also tells me I have another burf brewing.

I thank Mrs. Perfect Square and almost run into Earl as I push open the door.

"Mr. Sherlock, there is a phone call for you," Earl reports with some urgency.

• Chapter Twelve •
Tightening the Screws

"Did they find the ring?" I blurt out, seeing myself look hopeful and extremely damp in Earl's reflective lenses.

My heart soars at the thought that I can put this whole uncomfortable mess behind me and squeeze in some violin practice before my recital.

But Earl doesn't have to speak. The droop at the corner of his mouth tells me three things with just one look:

1. The ring hasn't been found.
2. Mr. Castro is on the phone and wants an update.
3. Earl's curious about the thing growing out of my forehead.

With a sigh, I climb through the door and slide into the back of the limo. I pick up the limo's sleek black phone.

"This is Sherlock," I squeak, feeling betrayed by my voice box once again.

"Please tell me you have the ring," Mr. Castro rumbles at me from the other end of the line.

"Not yet, Mr. Castro," I mumble. "But if I—"

"Sherlock," Mr. Castro interrupts. "The guests will start arriving in less than an hour. We're counting on you."

"Mr. Castro, detective work isn't like a cup

of instant soup. You have to—"

"And there's something else I didn't tell you," Mr. Castro interrupts again.

"Fantastic," I sigh. Mr. Castro is like a pitcher who only throws curveballs.

"The oversize diamond my son has misplaced originally belonged to the bride's great-great-great-grandmother. It's been in her family for over two hundred years. As you can imagine, the bride's family will be less than thrilled if they find out we lost their most prized family treasure. In fact, the news might cause a riot."

"For future reference, Mr. Castro, I don't need any more pressure."

"I just want you to keep an eye on the clock," he says.

"Mr. Castro, I'm a detective, not a magician who can pull fluffy white birds out of his sleeve whenever he feels like it!"

"I understand," he says as if he's suddenly distracted. "Has anybody located the florist yet?" he bellows at somebody.

"Mr. Castro, if you could just—" I look down at the phone. It has gone dead. Mr. Castro has hung up on me. Before I can feel bad about it, Earl stomps the gas pedal through the bottom of the vehicle. I am slammed back into the seat. I whip a seatbelt around me and click it in place faster than you can say "severe concussion."

Perhaps the act of fearing for your life speeds up time, because we come to a screeching halt in what feels like only a few seconds.

"Ralph's Chili Dog Palace?" I groan.

"Yes indeed. This is our second stop," Earl announces.

He jumps out, circles the car, and opens my door. "Mr. Sherlock, please hurry. I must pick up the bride and her bridesmaids in just sixty minutes."

"I'm detecting as fast as I can," I sigh as I make my way to the door. I stop momentarily and pull out my time line. I quickly jot down "Ralph's Chili Dog Palace" just to the right of "Mr. Spiffy's Tuxedo Emporium." My time line is starting to take shape. I stuff it back into my coat pocket, realizing I still have mountains to move.

Trust me, all eyes lock onto a kid who steps from a black stretch limousine and into a Ralph's Chili Dog Palace. My wet, too-small suit and lumpy forehead might also help explain all the staring.

I should mention here that "palace" is not the right word to describe this smelly hut. It occurs to me that Sherlock Holmes wouldn't be caught dead in a dump like this. Besides, The Great Detective wasn't known for his love of chili dogs. In fact, he only seemed to drink tea and nibble on the occasional scone, which looks like a combination of a donut, a muffin, and quick-dry cement.

There are just six small tables and every chair is filled. There must be twenty-seven eyes staring directly at me in utter silence.

"Um, I am trying to solve a mystery," I announce as loudly as I can, since they all look like they're waiting for me to say something.

"Are you trying to find out who stole the bottom of your pants?" some joker says from the back corner. This must be the kind of humor that chili dog lovers find hilarious, because the place erupts in laughter.

It's at this moment I catch a whiff of the

sickening breeze blowing out of the cramped kitchen. My stomach starts dancing a jig. I think I turn a shade of lime green, because the place grows eerily quiet again.

"I'm here to find a ring that has been lost!" I shout in desperation as I feel the chance of solving this mystery slipping between my toes. "Anyone who finds it will get as many chili dogs as they can eat for a whole year."

Perhaps they think I'm a rich kid because of the limo. Maybe they just want to get rid of me before I get sick right in the middle of the restaurant. But before I know it, they are all crawling around on the floor looking for the ring. If it's here, they'll find it.

The pimply guy wearing a paper hat behind the front counter pulls out a shoe box with "Lost and Found" written on the side. I glance inside. I see a rabbit's foot on a chain, some sunglasses, a pink glove, and a pair of wax

lips. I honestly don't expect to find a priceless two-hundred-year-old diamond ring in there, but I do consider borrowing the rabbit's foot. I could use the luck.

I notice everyone has completed their search. The energy and excitement has drained out of the room. They have returned to their chili dogs.

I scratch out my home number on a paper napkin and hand it to the pimply guy with the paper hat. "Call me if anything should turn up," I say. I exit without another word.

"Wait a second, kid," he calls after me. But I don't stop. I simply don't have the time . . . or the stomach for it.

• Chapter Fourteen •
Road Warrior

Riding a wave of growing frustration, I burst out of the back of the limo and into Edna's Travel Spot, the next stop on our magical mystery tour. Apparently, the groom came by this morning to pick up the tickets for his honeymoon.

The woman who greets me from behind the service counter is clearly scared of me. I must look like a wild boar with short pants on.

I figure that this woman must be Edna, because she has a big red splotch on her forehead, which is probably why she named this place Edna's Travel Spot.

Luckily for me, the space in front of Edna's counter is a small one. And Mr. Castro's son would not have gone behind it. I give the seating area in front of the counter a

thorough examination. I find nothing but a moldy, half-eaten gummy bear.

I hand Edna the gummy bear and thank her for her cooperation, which despite my low mood does make me sound a bit like a detective.

"I hope it's not that ring he's lost," Edna says as I turn to leave.

"What?" I gasp, quickly returning to the counter.

Her eyes grow wide. She can tell from my reaction that it's the ring that I'm searching for. "Oh dear, that diamond was as big as a golf ball."

"Wait!" I yelp. "You saw the ring today?"

"Yes, it was beautiful," she says quietly, finally understanding the kind of rabbit I'm trying to pull out of a hat. She suddenly looks at me like I'm a stone caught between a rock and a harder place. And I can't argue with her on that one. "I'm sorry I can't be more help," she says.

"Believe it or not, you've been a great help!" I say as I back out the door. I suddenly feel like a hound dog who's picked up a fresh scent. Or perhaps it's just my shirt that's starting to mildew. Either way, I'm hot on the trail of the missing monkey-eye diamond!

I pull out my time line and add Edna's Travel Spot. I put a diamond shape next to it. If the groom showed the ring to Edna, then the ring was lost *after* he was here. I must be getting close! And my time line is leading me straight to it.

I get a tingling feeling on the back of my

neck that usually means I'm close to solving a case. I haven't had this feeling since I found a missing stamp from my dad's rare stamp collection stuck to the bottom of one of his slippers.

Earl interrupts my tingling. "You have another urgent phone call."

This time I don't know what to expect.

Chapter Fifteen

On the Road Again

"Mom just came by the Castros' house looking for you," Hailey's voice informs me when I pick up the phone.

"Are you kidding me?" I thunder into the phone.

There's sort of an unwritten rule among detectives: Your mom is not supposed to bug you when you're on a case. Just imagine if Sherlock Holmes's mom was always interrupting him during his cases because he forgot his lunch or didn't make his bed. It's called an unwritten rule because it's supposed to be so dang obvious nobody bothers to waste a piece of paper on it.

"Mom said Mrs. Hudson dropped by our house to see if you were practicing for tonight's recital," Hailey tells me. "She told Mom you're her most challenging student."

"Well, I'm sort of busy right now," I huff into the phone. "I'm trying to solve a mystery in the time it takes for most people to make toast." While I say this, I'm sliding from left to right on the backseat of the limo. I'm so irritated by Hailey's news, I forgot to buckle up before Earl hit the gas. I grab a handle on the ceiling just above the door with my free hand and swing around like a monkey in a storm.

"Mom also said she can't find your violin,"

Hailey informs me.

"It's probably under my bed," I say.

"Nope. She looked there."

"Did she look in the bathroom?" I ask.

"The bathroom? You are so weird," she whispers. "Mom said she's looked everywhere. She wanted to know what kind of detective can never find anything."

"I hardly ever lose anything—"

Hailey interrupts me with a loud snort. "Sherlock, Mom told me some guy from Ralph's Chili Dog Palace just called our house to say that you left your clip-on tie there. We can only hope you're still wearing pants!"

I look down and notice for the first time that my tie is gone. The pressure of this case is getting to me. At least my pants are still in good standing.

"And talk about awkward," Hailey continues in a hushed voice. I am powerless to stop her. "I think Mom was wondering why she wasn't invited to this wedding. She's been a good neighbor to the Castros for a fragillion years. So I gave her a piece of wedding cake to cheer her up."

"Dang it, Hailey, stay away from that

cake!" I shout just as the limo comes to a sudden, jerking stop and the arm I'm dangling from is almost separated from the rest of my body. "Look, I don't have time for wedding gossip right now. I gotta go!"

"Hey, did you see that ice sculpture of a mongoose?" she whispers.

"That's supposed to be a swan," I say, rolling my eyes.

"Not a swan from my planet," she says. "Isn't it just awful?"

"I thought it was a weasel," I admit quietly.

"Mom thought it was a tree frog," she says breathlessly.

"Look, I don't have time for the mystery of the lumpy ice sculpture right now!" I explode in frustration.

"Oh, but you have time to stuff your big mouth at Ralph's Chili Dog Palace?" she explodes back.

"How did you even get this number?" I holler.

But the phone is dead.

Earl swings my door open. "Looks like someone has a neckwear mystery," he says with a chuckle.

"Neckwear?" I stare at Earl like I'm a stuffed fox in a natural history museum. My brain feels like a cell phone searching for a signal. Then it hits me that he's talking about my tie. "Earl, there are mysteries everywhere you turn," I say with just a hint of irritation as I crawl out the door.

Earl has a good laugh at that one.

At least somebody's having a good time on this wild goose chase.

Chapter Sixteen

Running on Empty

Our next three stops are my best chance to find a diamond in the rough. But each stop will gobble up precious time—and time is something I just don't have time to waste.

I notice immediately that Walt's Old-time Barber Shop has a very hairy floor. Three old men with extremely short hair just stare at my head with dreamy, milky eyes. The one who I assume is Walt lets me quickly sweep the floor, which I think might uncover something. It doesn't. I leave before the trio of barber zombies can attack my hair with their gleaming snippers.

After Walt's Old-time Barber Shop, we hit the Sock Barn. Unfortunately, today is their Annual Barn-burner Sock Blowout. The crowd is enormous, and I am just glad to get out of there alive. While I'm talking to the manager, Earl manages to buy a six-pack of dress socks for the price of a slice of cheese pizza. As you can imagine, I have trouble getting as giddy as Earl seems to be about his big sock score.

Helga's Palm Reading Shop is next. This place makes me so uneasy that I start murmuring like a crazy violin teacher.

Helga's eyes widen when she sees me. I must look like the ultimate client. Let's face it, with my preshrunk suit covered with gray hair, a lumpy forehead, no tie, a moist shirt, and a cornered-hamster look in my eyes, Helga's just licking her chops to see what bad things await in my future. I feel my internal creepometer blow a gasket. After a speedy look around, I burst out the door, despite Helga's offer of a "freebie" look into my future.

"Just one more stop," Earl says as we pull away from Helga's.

Never in my wildest dreams had I imagined that a groom on his wedding day could be so busy. As I slump all alone in the limo's elegant rear cabin, I stare at my now detailed time line and can't help but feel my confidence drain away.

Maybe I'm not cut out for this business. Maybe my teacher, Miss Piffle, is right; she says I should just give up on all this detective nonsense.

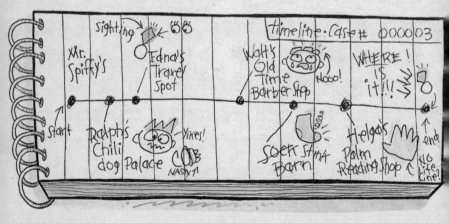

This case feels like a treasure hunt without the big red X at the end. It's like playing hide-and-seek when you don't realize that your friends have already gone home for dinner. It's like spending all day trying to find your favorite T-shirt, not knowing your dad used it to put out a kitchen grease fire.

I stare out the window and watch the homes and shops of Baskerville zip by. I must have missed something.

I flip the page in my notebook and write a list of all the places I've been. I review it carefully and wait for something to jump out at me. Nothing does. I make a list of all the people who have seen the ring today. There's not a likely thief among them.

I'm haunted by the fact that the ring was right under my nose at some point during this crazy chase, and I missed it. I have a nagging suspicion that the ring is not lost or stolen, just misplaced—and that's a significant difference. Still, a nagging suspicion isn't enough to solve a case.

I rest my lopsided forehead on the cool window and run the whole day through my head again and again. It's a lot like watching someone fall down a flight of stairs over and over.

"Last stop, Mr. Sherlock," Earl says, leaning through the door and tapping me on the shoulder. I'm so wrapped up watching my confidence plunge into a death spiral, I haven't even noticed that we've stopped.

I can tell some of the spring has gone out of Earl's step. His suit seems a little less starched. Even the mirrors of his sunglasses seem to have dimmed. "This is the end of the rainbow, I'm afraid," he says with a crooked smile.

Well, there's either a pot of gold waiting for me, or a pot of beef stew with lima beans and broccoli.

• Chapter Seventeen •
Last Chance for Gas

"You're on your own," Earl tells me, looking around at the quiet neighborhood we find ourselves standing in.

"I understand," I say awkwardly. "Thanks for the ride."

"I've only got seven minutes to pick up the bride and the bridesmaids and rush them to the Castros' house. But after that I can swing by here and pick you up, if you'd like. Here's my cell number. It's not a problem." Earl hands me his business card with his cell-phone number written in pen on the back.

When I look up from his card, Earl is gone. The limo suddenly rockets away from the curb and roars down the street.

I'm standing in front of Herbert Junior's tiny, empty home. It's on Doyle Street. It's only about half a mile from my house. I know this because there's a girl in my class named Sharon Sheldon who lives a few doors down from this house. But that's a whole other ball of earwax.

After we left Helga's Palm Reading Shop, I'd asked Earl to slow down to the legal speed limit for a few minutes so I could look around the back of the limo in case the ring was somehow stuck in the seat or under the carpet. Nothing.

While I searched, Earl told me that Mr.

Castro and his son spent about twenty minutes at this house. Earl explained that the two men went into the kitchen for only a few moments. Then they briefly played catch on the front lawn to work off some anxiety.

Now Earl is gone, and I'm alone.

I spend a few moments crawling around on the grass like a guy who lost a contact lens—while praying that Sharon Sheldon doesn't

happen to come wan-
dering by.

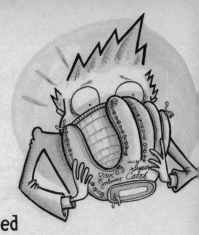

I also search every
inch around the small
front porch, since Earl
said the two men draped
their coats on the porch's railing while they
tossed the ball around. I even examine the
two baseball gloves still resting on the porch.
Nothing. Zippo. Nada.

I can't see into the front windows because
of the closed curtains, so I decide to jump the
fence and get a look into the kitchen through
the side window.

Little do I know that my fence-hopping
stunt will almost turn *me* into a missing-
person case.

• Chapter Eighteen •
Squeeze Play

I'm too short to see through the kitchen window—just one of the many drawbacks of being a kid detective.

In the tall weeds I find a rusted-out bucket, which I drag over to the kitchen window. Stepping up on the bucket, I peer inside. The house is completely empty and scrubbed clean. The only things I can see are two half-empty bottles of soda sitting near the kitchen sink. As I pull on the window's screen to see if it will come loose, I hear a noise behind me that turns my brain to jelly.

GRRRRRRRRRRRRR!

Without turning to look, I know the growl I hear belongs to Mr. Castro's monstrous, man-eating dog, Ranger.

He said Ranger was at a relative's house! And sure, his son is a sort of relative, but there is nothing more dangerous to a detective than fuzzy information. I close my eyes and realize this must be Mr. Castro's final curveball.

For as long as I can remember, I have feared Ranger like a tree fears a wood chipper. This dog would like nothing more than to eat my legs and save my arms for dessert.

Before my jellied brain can even consider my options, my legs take charge. They jump off the bucket and race through the dry weeds so fast, I think the sparks flying out of my heels might light them on fire.

I nearly clear the top of the fence before

Ranger's teeth snap onto the sleeve of my coat like a bear trap. The fence wobbles as the weight of Ranger's immense body catches up with his teeth.

And for the first time today, luck is on my side.

The mother of all burfs explodes into the back of my throat. It's a biggie. A whopper. The rotten gas rushes almost directly from my mouth into the beast's snarling snout. Jinxed by his highly tuned sense of smell, Ranger lets me go with a yowl, and I drop safely onto the other side of the fence.

He's taken half the right sleeve of my suit. As I listen to him tear the fabric to bits on the other side of the fence, my eyes fall onto the front porch—where Mr. Castro and his son hung their jackets while they tossed the ball around and worked off a little nervous energy.

Then, as if by some unseen magical fairy dust, I unexpectedly have a good idea where the ring is. It's only a hunch. An inkling. A deep pass into the back of the end zone with no time left on the clock. But it's all I've got.

Perhaps the fall from the fence has jarred the idea loose in my head. Maybe it was coming just inches away from becoming a pile of dog bones. I don't know. All I know is, I'm about to break the world record in the half-mile sprint.

• Chapter Nineteen •
The Flying Detective

As I turn onto Baker Street, there's no doubt in my mind that my mini-man pants are cramping my style. Or maybe it's the added wind resistance of my lumpy forehead. Heck, it could be that my near-death experience at the jaws of Ranger has drained some of the jet fuel from my legs. Whatever the reason, I'm setting no world records today. But I am still making pretty good time.

My legs are flying on autopilot. I let them do what they do best and focus my mind on what I'll have to do upon reaching the Castros' home.

I blaze past my house and see my parents and sisters waiting for me in our driveway. My mom is holding my violin case. My dad is on his cell phone, probably calling the Castros' house to find out what happened to me.

"There he goes!" I hear Hailey exclaim as I sprint past them. "He looks crackers!" she shrieks.

As I approach the Castros' house, I see Earl leaning on the trunk of the limo. He pops up when he sees me, but I am past him before he can think of anything to say.

I take the stairs of the Castros' front porch in a single bound and come through the open door at full speed.

In an instant, I take in the scene.

I hear elegant string music. I smell roast beef. Through the open back door, I see the glum-looking groom and his groomsmen in the backyard, waiting for the bride in front of a large crowd. Irene Adler is walking down the center aisle flinging flower petals all over the place like a nutcase.

Without slowing down, I aim toward Mr. Castro, who is on the other side of the room.

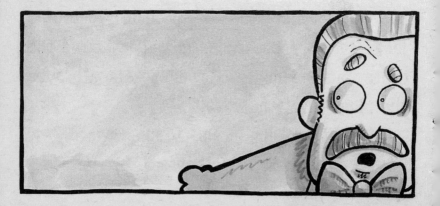

He has pulled a woman in a puffy white dress to the side. The bride! Her bridesmaids nervously huddle just a few feet away. "I have some bad news to tell you about the ring," Mr. Castro says to the bride just before I crash every ounce of myself into his shoulder.

The weight of my body is only a tiny fraction of Mr. Castro's massive frame, but I have the element of surprise going for me. Not only that, I am easily moving faster than a speeding bullet. Plus, I give my launch a little extra oomph because I know that if the bride hears about the missing ring, she'll

start to blubber all over the place. I don't want to be responsible for that.

Mr. Castro and I go down in a heap of legs and arms. The bride yelps. A few of the bridesmaids gasp. Mr. Castro makes a noise that sounds like somebody just got kicked in the bagpipes.

Before he can sit up, I stuff my hand deep into the giant breast pocket of Mr. Castro's tuxedo jacket. When I pull my hand out, the diamond ring gleams at the end of my trembling fingers. The diamond *is* as big as a monkey's eye!

Mr. Castro is so shocked by the ring's sudden appearance that he can't speak. He looks like he's just been hit in the head by a flying detective.

"After you and your son played catch earlier, you must have taken his jacket by accident," I wheeze, trying to catch my breath. He doesn't react to the news. "You and your son simply switched jackets without knowing it. It's so simple, it's complicated."

"I had the ring?" Mr. Castro whispers, gazing bug-eyed at the sparkling ring.

"It was an honest mistake, Mr. Castro," I say. "Now snap out of it! There isn't a moment to lose."

I snatch a pillow off the couch, place the massive ring on it, and hobble out the back door. For pete's sake, I'm the ring bearer after all!

As I teeter down the center aisle, it's clear from all the "ooohs" and "aaahs" that Mr. Castro's guests have never seen anything like me at a wedding before. I hear Irene Adler burst into laughter somewhere.

Before I know it, the openmouthed groom is taking the ring slowly off the pillow like he can't believe his eyes—or his luck.

I think he's too stunned and relieved to say anything. And honestly, I'm just glad to save this case at the buzzer.

As I make my way back toward the house, I pass the bridesmaids, who have started filing down the aisle. I slip past Mr. Castro, who just stares at me. He looks like he's starting to cry—I've heard weddings do that to people.

I'd love to stick around and get lots of handshakes, pats on the back, and carrot cake, but I have a violin recital to go to.

• Chapter Twenty •
Rolling to the Rescue

Earl insists on driving my family to my recital in style.

I agree, on the condition that he lock the ice bucket in the trunk.

My family asks me lots of questions about what happened. But I'm too tired to give the details of how I located the missing monkey-eye diamond. Besides, I'm not sure if they'd even believe me.

My dad slips off his tie and ties it around my neck in something he calls a double Windsor knot. I like the name because it sounds like the kind of knot Sherlock Holmes would use.

My mom insists that I not wear my too-tight coat. She takes it from me and examines the ripped end of the sleeve with a puzzled look on her face. But thankfully, she doesn't ask me about it.

I'm no longer worried about my upcoming performance. I'll just do what I can do. Besides, I'm more certain than ever that I wasn't born to be a violinist; I was born to be a detective.

Dear Sherlock,

My dad filled me in on how you saved the day in the nick of time. (Good tackle!) It turned out to be the best day of my life. Thank you from both of us! You are a miracle worker!

Herbert Jr.

P.S. PLEASE KEEP THIS WHOLE MESS HUSH HUSH!

MAUI
OCT 13
HAWAII

Sherlock
221 Baker St.
Baskerville